The Snakeman Cometh

Allison Pollack Alexander

PublishAmerica
Baltimore

First printing

Photo of Linda Martin by Aimee Keeney-Fisher

ISBN: 1-59286-962-9
PUBLISHED BY
PUBLISHAMERICA, LLLP.
www.publishamerica.com
Baltimore

Printed in the United States of America

Also by Allison Pollack Alexander

Return To Suicide

Dance of the Misbegotten

For John, Rosie, Jeremy and Joe

Many thanks to Judi Jackson, Linda Martin, Jeanne Ackerman, Aimee Keeney-Fisher, Brad Fisher, Tammy Brook, Susan Greene, Kristine Southworth (the folks at Artful Gatherings) and "Jackie".

1

"We are counted as sheep for the slaughter..."

On a Sunday in August, the snakeman came to town.

The two hundred and twelve inhabitants of the backwater hollow of Pine Mountain flocked to the church to see for themselves the man who could stare down poisonous snakes and handle them unharmed.

He'd promised to deliver great and mighty wonders from God, and although he stood just above five feet, there was something about his light blue eyes and the conviction with which he spoke, that made people stop and listen.

It was a strange day. Gray thunderclouds rolled across the sky faster than usual, sending a hot swirling wind through the empty streets, in a town cut off from the world on all four sides by the ridges of the Cumberland Mountains at the eastern tip of The Daniel Boone Nation Forest.

Unlike any other Sunday, the straight-backed pews of the tiny church were packed shoulder-to-shoulder. The women, in flowered cotton dresses that reached well below the knee, fanned themselves with whatever they had on hand to serve that purpose.

Men, in their high-topped shoes, stood at the back of the church, their coal-dust stained hands clasped behind their backs. There was not a necktie worn amongst them.

Children of all ages were sprinkled about, sitting on their mother's knees, in arms, or standing, shifting restlessly from one foot to the other.

Praise and song were under way when George and Bonnie Mosley came shuffling in with their three children. As they stood at the back of the church, the two Mosley boys, twelve-year-old Arliss and eleven-year-old Buddy craned their necks to have a look.

The daughter, Jolene, a coltish ten-year-old, held her father's hand and yawned. The excitement that arose from the citizens of the sleepy mining town meant only one thing to the girl. Her favorite book, *Tess of the d'Urbervilles* would have to wait. Jolene was on page forty-three when her father poked his head into her room, telling her to get ready for church.

She rolled on her back, put the book over her face and said, "I don't want to go! I want to stay here."

"You'll go to church, come hell or high water, and it may be both!"

George wasn't beyond taking the strap to his only daughter, and he did, often. He was raised in a house where children were seen and not heard. Jolene made herself heard, loud and clear.

"You be ready in ten minutes, or I'll strap you good," he said as he turned away.

"You shouldn't *force* someone to go to church," she called after him.

That stopped him dead in his tracks, bringing him back to her door. "What did you say?"

"You shouldn't force me," she said flatly, thinking a strapping was sure to come. She wasn't afraid.

"This is a God-fearing house. You want to turn away from the Lord, you do it when you is grown and gone. Now get up and get ready or you'll get the strapping of your life!"

Later, as the family walked together down Main Street, the lanky George turned to his wife. "Bonnie, the girl spends too much time readin'. She's got all kinds of ideas put in 'er head from them books. Doesn't even wanna go to church no more."

Jolene glanced at her mother with a frown. It wasn't something she liked to hear, but she did, often.

As his father before him, George had gone straight from his mother's apron strings into the mines, settling into a coal-camp house alongside the railroad tracks. What was the use in book learning if it didn't put food on the table?

Dank underground tunnels, vertical shafts and steel augers were all he knew or cared to know. He paid his rent to the Hughs Coal Company, bought his goods from the company store, and with that, he was satisfied. For him, nothing else existed beyond the dense hardwood hollows of the county line.

"All that readin'll get her to college someday," Bonnie said, trying to understand a daughter whose dreams reached beyond their world.

Worn-looking at 29, Bonnie was a typical miner's wife. She too never ventured but a stone's throw from Pine Mountain, where all there was for a girl to do was to marry a miner, bear him children and hope the "black lung" didn't leave her widowed too soon.

"My teacher says I'm the best reader she's ever had in her class." Jolene left her mother's side and walked beside her father.

"I can read Thomas Hardy books, Pa. *Thomas Hardy*," she said.

It meant nothing to him.

"Thomas Hardy, smomas pardy, who gives a rat's tail!" Arliss walked backwards in front of Jolene.

"You're just jealous." Without taking her eyes from her brother, she searched for her father's hand with hers, but he was still angry and brushed it away.

She expected at any time for Arliss to reach for a handful of her hair, twist and pull as she struggled. The two siblings would then call for Buddy to intervene.

Naturally, he sided with Arliss every time, leaving the girl to fend for herself. Any other little girl would have been left in tears, but not Jolene Mosley. She knew Arliss wanted to make her cry, so she held back her tears in stubborn battle after stubborn battle.

"You waste time readin' when you ought be in the kitchen helpin' your ma," George said, curling his fingers around his daughter's hand when she reached for him again. "Arliss, turn 'round and leave her be."

She walked the rest of the way beside her father, who in profile matched her gentle overbite and longish features.

Singing reached the family's ears as the steeple came into view at the bottom of the hill.

George said, "You made us late, Jolene."

Nudging their way inside, they saw him for the very first time.

The Snakeman.

The Reverend Franklin B. Browning was at the alter, hands raised in the air. His thin arms quivered. The tiny church was alive with praise. Many in the congregation dropped to their knees, voices rising to a shrill.

Jolene held tightly to her father's hand, while her unruly brother's, tugging at their mother's dress, begged to be taken up front.

"Hush!" Bonnie said. "He ain't got a snake just yet!"

Suddenly the room fell into a hush as Reverend Browning opened the snake box that was next to the pulpit, producing two large rattlers. He held the writhing serpents in his right hand, high above his head, their rattler's batting side to side, faster and faster as they became more agitated, ready to strike.

With hands over mouths and hearts, eyes wide, the congregation watched.

"'*Behold!*'" he called out, "'*I give unto you power to tread on serpents and scorpions and over all the power of the enemy; and nothing shall by any means hurt you.*'"

12

He then brought the snakes down, holding them close to his face, closing his eyes, leading the worshippers in prayer.

When the people found their voices, their words came out like gibberish, in wails, as a lost child would, crying for its mother. And as they spoke in tongues, their bodies trembled.

The serpents' heads swayed, their forked tongues darting. Their tails shook in short movements, back and forth, shaking into a deafening roar. They writhed and hissed in his hands, rolling over one another like black ooze.

The temperature in the room rose, but the congregation didn't notice. Drenched in sweat, they rode the wave of whatever possessed them to submit to the stranger who rode into town two days prior, in a beat-up station wagon, with a pinched-face wife, a crateful of snakes, and God's word on his tongue.

The serpent display ended and Reverend Browning placed the snakes back in the box and descended the pulpit, stopping halfway down the aisle.

The congregation waited in silence for his next act of faith, his next utterance, his next movement. Their mouths salivated, as if they'd been dying of hunger all their lives, and having just been reminded how starved they'd been.

All eyes followed him.

"I feel," he said, low and threatening, "that there is amongst us a vessel of darkness! A tool of the devil! A child of God who needs to be delivered from Satan's grip!"

Placing his palm on his forehead, he slowly looked around the room. Scripture poured from his mouth, mingled with nonsensical words. In the momentary trance-like state, he quivered, sweat soaking his clothes.

They stared, waited, mouths hung open in awe. Even the smallest of children, who would have been squirming to be released from their mothers' laps, were silent.

Suddenly he stopped, froze perfectly still, took a step

forward and thrust his finger at Jolene Mosley.

A collective "Ahhhh" came from the crowd as he came toward the girl, who clung to her father's arm. Bonnie and George stepped aside as Browning approached their daughter and placed his hand on her forehead.

"Let him help you, Jolene,"George said as she looked up at him in horror.

Standing alone, she attempted to back away, shaking her head, but there was nowhere to go, except into a wall of bodies.

"I command ye Satan, in the name of our Lord Jesus, to come out of her!" Browning shouted.

Jolene stood ridged, then began to tremble under his cold, boney hand.

"The devil fights to remain in her! Can you feel it?" he said.

"Amen!" rose up in unison.

"Can you see it?"

"Un-huh, Lord Almighty!" they all cheered.

The church rocked with the chanting and weaving of the crowd, some raising their hands to Heaven, some dropping prostrate on the dirty wood planks.

All praying for the tortured soul of Jolene Mosley.

The girl jerked away, darting through the crowd, throwing elbows, dodging the prying hands that tried to keep her there. She tried to scream, but nothing escaped her open mouth.

Halfway up Main Street, she turned around to see Arliss and her father coming after her.

It was August 8th, 1944. The day the Snakeman came to town. The day the congregation was divided.

Some went home mesmerized by the man of small stature, who seemed to possess an enormous amount of faith and the power of God.

Others, once removed from the frenzy of the moment, felt it had the markings of a sideshow at the fair. How bizarre, for George Mosley and his eldest boy to drag that poor little girl back inside the church, digging her heels against the floor in resistance.

No amount of pleading on her part would move them to let her go. Not even her mother came to her aid.

The child was delivered to the Snakeman's feet, looking as if she'd suddenly gone mad, with bruised knees, and frightened eyes peering behind a veil of tangled hair. She cried to her mother for help.

Bonnie turned away, towards the Reverend, who said, "It's a good thing I've come. There's a devil amongst you in the purest form; a little girl."

One month later, forty-nine members of the Pine Hill Baptist Church helped the Reverend Franklin B. Browning erect "The True Believers Holiness Church", three miles south of Pine Mountain.

Cecile Hughes donated the land to the Reverend, finding him to be a true man of God.

2

Nine Years Later

They wore white cotton prayer bonnets tied loosely at the nape of their necks. They wore no make-up, and their uncut hair was pulled straight back from the forehead.

In single file they walked.

In single file, reciting Psalms in unison.

They spoke verse after verse in soft gentle voices; no one louder than the next, not stumbling over any words, as if each line was burned into their minds. In the curve of each elbow, they clutched crude wicker baskets.

In single file they walked, down a well-worn path that cut through the thickest part of the woods. Sometimes they could see the creek through the underbrush, but it would disappear again on its own winding way through the hills.

Agnes Browning was at the lead. Her once beautiful chestnut hair was now dull and brittle from washings with lye soap. Store-bought hair products were for the vain. The part down the middle of her head was uncommonly wide, and her hair was pulled back so tightly, it caused her eyebrows to arch slightly. Any smile that came from her mouth was close-lipped and tight, as if to stretch her mouth upward would be a testament to her lack of sobriety. She was a woman on a mission, in a permanent state of dispassion.

The psalms came forth from her like a war cry, a marching tune, as mothers, wives and daughters, twenty-six in all, droned on after her.

They swatted flies that desired their sweat, slammed their palms against their necks to squash mosquitoes; reciting, reciting, until they reached a clearing, where blackberries grew in abundance.

Agnes turned around to the line of women that meandered down the path. "Stick to your bush!"

The line quietly dispersed, and the berry picking began.

"Sister Jolene!" Agnes called out to a young woman, who lazily turned her whole body, revealing an uninterested expression in her hazel eyes.

"Sister Agnes?"

"Stick to your bush Sister Jolene. Skippin' around's a wasteful way to pick berries."

"Yes, ma'am."

"…and Sister Jolene…"

"Yes, ma'am…"

"Tuck those stray hairs up under your bonnet."

3

A dull windowless, clapboard structure served as the church building. Inside, there were no pews. Instead, chairs formed in a circle, and during service, Browning would place himself in the center, turning, pointing, and spewing scripture like venom from a snake.

Next to the church was a large hall, where on Wednesday nights they gathered for a communal dinner and a prayer meeting.

As every member of the True Believers had done, the Mosleys abandoned their tin-roofed, company-owned home in Pine Mountain to rebuild their lives amongst their brethren in the wooded hollow.

The communal buildings and homes of the faithful were set in the open air of fifty-foot white pines that roared with the slightest breeze. In the spring, the stately trees shed their pollen, covering everything underneath in a film of green.

In the fall, they discarded a portion of their needles, leaving the floor of the hollow in a soft, light brown bedding.

It was on one of those particular Wednesdays, in early summer, just after her nineteenth birthday, that Jolene Mosley sat on an overturned bucket on the back porch of the meeting hall, peeling potatoes.

She was halfway through the bushel when her mother called to her from the kitchen. "Aren't you done peelin'? The water's set to boil!"

"Just about, ma'am."

"What?"

"Just about, ma'am!"

"What? I can't hear you!"

Jolene sighed, got up from the stool and stood at the threshold of the kitchen. "Just about, ma'am!"

She returned to her place on the porch just as Agnes Browning came up the steps carrying a pan of hogmaw.

She turned and looked down at the girl bent over the potatoes. "Sister Jolene."

"Sister Agnes," Jolene replied without looking up.

Jolene was expecting a rebuke for being rude, but Agnes had already gone inside.

A small parade of fresh-faced young ladies followed. They were bonnet-clad, reserved, carrying with them various homemade dishes for the communal meal.

Jolene never lifted her eyes as she was greeted by each one, mumbling her replies, "Sister Mildred, Sister Anne, Sister Penny…" on and on till they all passed, disappearing inside, where their carefully worded chatter would stop once the table was set and the men arrived.

Jolene always volunteered for chores that left her isolated.

From her downward gaze, she saw a pair of men's boots, then lifted her eyes to the cold stare of her oldest brother.

Arliss, like Buddy, had their mother's strong Germanic features; stout and well built, honey-colored hair and blue eyes. The boys lumbered into manhood thick as oxen.

"Sister Jolene," he mocked.

She went on working without a reply.

"*I said*, Sister Jolene."

Again she ignored him.

"Ain't proper manners not to answer, *Sister Jolene.*" He glanced around to see if anyone was coming, as she peeled harder, gouging the paring knife deep into the meat of the potato.

Arliss swooped his hand down and grabbed the spud.

ALLISON POLLACK ALEXANDER

"Leave me be," she said. She reached up for it, but he tossed it away.

"Leave me alone. Ma wants these 'taters quick."

She took another from the bushel, gouging again, this time harder, accidentally slicing the blade into the tip of her thumb. She dropped everything at her feet and stuck the appendage into her mouth, sucking, tasting blood. It was a small cut, but it stung.

"See that?" he sneered.

She glanced up, frowning.

"God's tellin' you to listen to me," he said.

"This has nothing to do with God at all, now let me alone!"

"Jolene, times a wastin'!" her mother called out.

Relieved, the girl quickly stood up and lifted the heavy bucket, pushed past her brother with the swaying of her hip, and went inside, her waist-length ponytail swaying past her untied bonnet.

4

After supper, they sat in church, hands clasped together neatly on their laps. Expressionless, they waited while Browning stood in the center, fingers pinching the bridge of his nose.

He looked up and said, "*'This I say then... Walk in the Spirit, and ye shall not fulfill the lust of the flesh.'*"

He circled the room. "*'For the flesh lusteth against the Spirit, and the Spirit against the flesh.'*"

His mouth turned up slightly, in a half smile. "*'And these things are contrary one to the other.'*"

He stood before Jolene, who ran her sweaty palms down her legs, over her knees, then clasped them together.

His voice rose an octave. "*'And they which do such things, shall not, SHALL NOT I say, inherit the Kingdom of God.'* Sister Jolene, do you desire to inherit the Kingdom of God?"

All eyes were on the girl as she uttered a weak, "Yes, sir."

Browning turned to the crowd asking, "Does that sound like a woman of conviction?"

"No!" they shouted.

Browning let out a laugh and looked around at the congregation. "Sister Jolene, the works of the flesh were manifest in you yesterday."

She had no idea what he was talking about. Her eyes scanned the congregation of stern, unfriendly faces, who just moments before had greeted her with smiles and praise.

"And you have sinned mightily by lusting," Browning said.

Jolene shook her head in confusion. "What have I done this time?"

"Daughter of Eve, after berry picking, what happened to you?"

"I don't know," she replied.

"Think! Think! Your body manifested lust."

She tried to remember. She thought hard. He had called her a daughter of Eve, meaning she had committed a great sin. Then she remembered, or thought she had. After berry picking, the group descended from the hilltop. It was late afternoon, and the sun had moved behind the ridge. Her sweaty body became chilled, and her nipples protruded through her underclothes and dress.

"Was it my…" she looked down at her breasts, but dared not say the word.

Browning's tight lips formed into a little smile. "Yes, yes, indeed, it was. So you do know, and you were aware. Your body manifested lust, for which you'll be punished."

A moan came from her lips.

"You must, under all circumstances control yourself!"

"I…I was cold. I…I—"

With the snap of his fingers, Browning was handed a wooden cane. Jolene stood up.

"No!" she shouted. "I was cold!" She turned to her mother, groaning, "Mama! Help me!"

Bonnie turned away.

"Hush, Jolene!" George Mosley said. "The preacher done called you out!"

"Yes, Sister Jolene! Repent!" came cries from the crowd.

"I didn't sin! I was cold! Cold! Cold!" she screamed until her throat hurt, but her cries fell on ears that would not reason as they shouted in unison, reproaching her.

Seized at the wrists, the young woman was forcibly bent over a chair, her dress hiked up, exposing her underpants to the now frenzied crowd, who quivered and spoke in tongues. She struggled and strained as the cane came down hard on her buttocks and legs, burning and stinging her flesh. Turning her face away from her parents, who were in the thick of the furor, she screamed for mercy.

The men lined up to bring down God's judgment on her. Each took their turn striking her two or three times, and as they did, they would repeat, "*The way of the wicked is an abomination to the Lord.*"

The men of the Mosley household were among her tormentors, while the women prayed in the shadows, crying, weeping, some pounding their fists on the ground rebuking Satan.

Bonnie sat stoic, staring off into the distance, then remembering she may be called out for sitting silent, she lifted her hands to the sky and cried out to the Lord.

Browning took the cane after the last man in line had his turn. "Rise!" he commanded to Jolene.

Once upright, she began to sway, feeling dizzy and sick. She vomited, wiped her mouth with the back of her hand and looked up. Chanting faces blended together, Browning's prayer became muddled.

"Mama." She let out a moan before crumbling to the ground.

5

Russell Nash hitched a ride from Knoxville, Tennessee, down route 6, and got as far as Pine Mountain two days later, just before dusk.

As he stood in the road, miners from the Hughes Coal Company came drifting down the steep slope of Main Street, squinting at the remaining daylight, their tin lunch buckets swinging at their sides.

Russell approached the first one to reach him. "Hey, there. I'm lookin' for Reverend Browning's place! Mind pointin' me the way?"

The miner studied the road-worn stranger as the others caught up.

"What the hell you goin' up there for?"

"He's kin," Russell replied.

"Yer uncle's a fake preacher," one said.

A chorus of agreement rose up.

"All I did was ask someone to point me the way," Russell said.

"Three miles south," one offered. "Gravel road at the bottom of the holler."

"Much obliged." Russell turned to leave. Hushed voices followed him, but he walked on until he could hear them no more and the wooden houses that hugged the edge of the winding street gave way to scrub yards with broken fences, until finally he was out in the open, surrounded on either side by thick woods and open sky.

He reached The "True Believers" after dark, greeted by the

barrel of a shotgun with Agnes Browning at the other end of it.

"Aunt Agnes, don't shoot! It's me, Russell! Russell Nash."

"Russell's in prison."

"It's me, I swear!"

"Don't swear on God's land!" She hiked the barrel of the shotgun towards his forehead.

"It's me, Aunt Agnes. I can prove it!"

"Go 'head."

"Uncle Franklin was makin' moonshine back in Buckburn…"

"Franklin." She shook her husband out of sleep. "Yer nephew's downstairs."

"What? Who?" He shot straight up. "Russell?"

"Yup, Russell."

Browning threw on his trousers, grabbed a shirt that hung over the chair and hurried downstairs. Agnes followed him.

"Uncle Frank." Russell stood in the dimly lit foyer.

Browning stopped out of arms reach. "When'd ya get out, boy?" He was tight-lipped, cautious.

"Two months prior."

"How'd you find me?"

"It wasn't easy. Wasn't easy at all. Tracked down Nigel Bowles in Knoxville. He had a hunch you were somewhere in these parts of Kentucky. Said you were a preacher now. That true?"

Browning nodded, to which Russell laughed, "Why, if Sheriff Harley could see you now, why he'd bust a gut!"

"Sheriff Harley made five dollars every time he turned our still in," Browning replied, not amused.

"Yeah, but he let us build it again, and again. Those were some crazy times."

It was evident Russell's recollections of days gone by were not welcome. He suddenly felt uncomfortable.

"Sit down, boy," Browning said.

Russell stepped into the main part of the house and sat on the sofa, across from Browning, who sat on an over-stuffed chair and asked sharply, "What you want?"

"I got nowhere to go." He shrugged. "Thought there'd be a place for me here, to start over."

"There's nothing here for you, boy. Shoulda stayed up in Knoxville where there's work."

"I spent twenty years doin' time for something I'm not sure I did. I figured you'd at least give me a place to come back to." As he spoke, his face reddened, his neck tensed up.

"You did it, son, no doubt."

"We were all shootin' that night. Could of been your bullet, could of been Nigel's. No tellin'."

Browning leaned forward. "Didn't you already go to trial for this, and weren't you found guilty? Or did you miss something these last, what, twenty years?"

"Guess it was easy to pin it on me, wasn't it, Uncle Frank?"

Browning glared at Russell with malevolence. "You'd best watch your step."

"Look here, I don't want trouble—"

"Good thing, 'cause we don't talk about those days. Got that understood? My moonshine days are over and done with."

"We don't need you stainin' our good name. Franklin and me, we've seen God and we don't live in sin no more," Agnes said.

"So, we're just gonna forget it all happened? Just like that? Twenty years?" Russell replied.

"You want them years back? It don't work that way. Those were the times we lived in. See, son, the devil ruled those hills in them days, and what happened, happened."

Browning pressed his fingertips against his closed eyelids, then looked up glassy-eyed, saying, "*Say not thou, I will recompense evil; but wait on the Lord, and He shall save thee—*'"

"What?"

"'—*for I am come not to call the righteous, but the sinners to repentance.*'"

Russell made another attempt to get his point across. "I served time for something I may not have done. Don't you understand?"

"'*What shall I do for you? And wherewith shall I make the atonement, that ye may bless the inheritance of the Lord?*'"

Russell looked his uncle square in the eyes. "You gonna answer me with Bible talk all night long?"

Browning leaned into him, veins bulging from his neck. "'*In the latter days, perilous times shall come*—'"

Russell rolled his eyes, sighed, then moved to get up, but Browning took him firm by the forearm.

"The latter days, boy, *the latter days!* The Lord calls me with His Endtime message, and I'm to say, 'Sorry, Lord, I need to redeem my nephew?' The Lord will redeem you, boy, not me! Not me! I've seen God, and I know He will redeem you!"

He turned to his wife. "Agnes, get Russell here a clean towel and show 'em the spare bed."

She disappeared down the hall.

"Get some rest, and we'll talk come morning. I have a lot to share. No, I can't give you those years back, but I can give you something better."

Browning stood up and reached for Russell's hand. "The Lord will redeem thee, boy. I don't have the power."

Russell was tired, and the thought of sleeping in a decent bed was appealing, so he shook Browning's hand, said nothing and went down the hall.

6

Jolene stepped carefully with her bare feet as she made her way through the dense, shadowy forest, down towards the creek. She stopped short when she heard laughter. A group of boys were fishing. Her brothers, no doubt were among them.

Sitting on her haunches, she spied on them, wishing they'd go away so she could dip her feet in the cool water. It was a muggy day, with haze hanging below the treetops, to where one could barely make out the surrounding mountains. Though somewhat cooler, not even the deep hollow could escape the summer's heat.

A heavy hand on her shoulder brought her to her feet. Arliss had crept up the path behind her.

"What you doin' all sneaky back here?" he said.

"You boys always get the good part of the creek."

"What do you want down here anyhow? You're supposed to be making quilts at the hall."

"Who wants to make quilts? Besides, when's it your business?"

She wanted to poke fun at his scattered whiskers that were supposed to be his beard and sideburns. Instead, she turned away from him. He reached for her.

"Let go of my arm!"

He cocked his head, grinning.

She jerked away, surprised she'd broken his grip, and took off running towards home. He was soon at her heels. She was thrown to the ground, her shoulders pinned beneath his knees.

"I can't breath!" she cried.

He laughed. "I don't give a good God damn!"

Her eyes grew wide. "You cursed!"

"So what? Shit, fuck, damn." He lowered his head to her ear. "Cunt."

So many times he'd wrestled his sister to the ground, away from the eyes of the community. He would always let her go after she'd wiggled and fussed so much and he'd grown bored.

This time his breath was on her neck. He stretched his body over hers, his full weight down. She froze beneath him. This new game. This new torment. His body rhythmically pushing into hers.

She screamed into his hand that was firmly over her mouth. The more she screamed, the harder he pushed, until she tasted blood on her lip.

He relaxed, panting into her hair, then let her wiggle out from under him. He rolled on his back and looked up at her. She stood there, eyes open wide, staring at his upturned mouth, where a laugh escaped.

Jolene ran through the woods, feeling her knees might buckle at any time, wiping tears and saliva with a shaking hand she couldn't still.

She turned. No, he hadn't followed. She turned again as she ran, running, barreling into something.

Russell Nash.

There were never any strangers in the hollow, ever. He was just as surprised to have this wet-faced, young woman come tumbling into him.

As she stared, mouth half-opened, he started to say, "You all right?"

But she had maneuvered out of his path, and after stumbling over herself a bit, she ran out of sight.

7

She found her mother napping. Thinking to wake her, tell her. Daughter of Eve, what is there to tell?

Your breasts heave and tighten when Browning handles the snakes. So what is there to tell?

Goosebumps spread down your arms and over your soft belly in waves.

Alone in the night, you ache between your legs, but dare not touch, because somehow he'll know, and call you out.

Daughter of Eve, what is there to tell that won't get turned back on you?

She stood in the airless heat of her room, pulling her dress up over her head. Her large feet pressed against the dark wood floor, her naked body barely visible in the windowpane, which served as the only reflection of herself she could find.

No mirrors were allowed at The True Believers. It was the ultimate form of vanity, to admire one's reflection, and the human body in all its functions, was sinful and dirty. Dirty like hers.

Even the innocent act of holding her father's hand was no longer her pleasure, since the day she first bled.

She was suddenly diseased.

"Am I gonna die?" the twelve-year-old Jolene had asked her mother.

"No, no, you ain't gonna die. You're comin' into womanhood, that's all."

"I don't like the napkin. It feels funny."

"It don't matter if you like it or not. You have to wear it.

Now come, quit your murmuring, or I'll set you to prayer 'till tomorrow!"

"My belly hurts."

Bonnie sighed and took her skinny girl by the shoulders and tried best she could to explain. "We're the Daughters of Eve, and we pay the price of her sins, '...*she took of the fruit thereof, and did eat, and God said unto the woman, I will greatly multiply thy sorrow...*'"

The girl protruded her lower lip at her mother.

"What, child?"

"What if I don't want to be a woman?"

"Well, you can't stay a little girl."

"Why not?"

"Don't be foolish."

"I don't want womanhood, Ma. It doesn't feel good. My belly hurts."

"You were born female, an' you'll follow God's will for it." Affectionately, she stroked her daughter's hair, "You'll get married, bear babies and honor your husband. All the things a woman was born to do."

"Ma, I don't want a husband!"

"Child, many things we don't want in this life, but we do them."

"Why? What if I want to do something else?"

"Jolene, you're being foolish, and '*foolishness is bound in the heart of a child—*'"

The girl sighed, "'—*but the rod of correction will drive him far from it.*' I don't want a whoppin', Ma."

"Then mind your thoughts!"

Jolene remembered that day well, and all the other days she would ask her mother questions. They were usually answered with a day confined to the prayer room; a dark, airless closet, where her eyes would strain by candlelight to memorize scripture that fit the offense.

She held the crumpled dress in her hand, shaken, disgusted that Arliss had rubbed himself against it, leaving a stain. She crammed it under her mattress, crawled on her knees to the corner of her bedroom, curled into a fetal position, repeating, "*...your inward part is full of ravening and wickedness....*"

"*...your inward part is full of ravening and wickedness....*"

"*...your inward part is full of ravening and wickedness....*"

A short time later, her mother found her there, still whimpering scripture. She led Jolene to the prayer room, and when George came home from a meeting of the Elders, he whipped his daughter for being absent from the hall, where all the unmarried women were to be that day.

At supper, she sat across from Arliss without ever looking up. Each mouthful of food stung the little cut inside her lower lip and her eyes were puffy from crying. Twice the boy got up from the table to get something and made certain to pass behind her, rubbing his finger along her back.

Jolene didn't look up to see if her parents noticed. She didn't want to look at her father, who whipped her harder than he ever had before.

"Jolene, eat," her mother said.

"I'm trying."

"You won't *try*. You *will*," George said. "Look at me when I's talkin' to you!"

She lifted her eyes to her father's angry face.

"And the way the devil has a hold on you, you best go to the meetings where you ought to be and not run off by yerself."

"Yes, sir," she replied, seeing Arliss from the corner of her eye, grinning smugly, trying not to laugh.

8

"I ain't never seen rattlers this big." Russell was in one of the many outbuildings that dotted the woods. He was bent down, looking into the snake cages.

"Biggest in these parts," Browning replied.

"That bite'll kill you in a skinny minute."

"I only hold 'em when the Lord tells me it's all right to do it. If I do it on my own account, well, sure, I'll get bit." Browning led Russell out the door. They walked towards the meeting hall.

"Only True Believers should handle poisonous snakes. It's when you take your mind off the Lord." He slapped his hands together. "That's when they get ya! Don't ever take your mind off the Lord."

"Shoot, I don't know how to get my mind on the Lord, not that it matters any."

Browning turned to his nephew, taking him by the shoulders. "You will, in time. Stay close to me. I'll teach you the way."

There was a buzz of activity preparing for the "social". Russell and Browning stopped just short of the back porch.

"Them snakes ever killed anyone up here?"

"Five so far," Browning replied.

The thought made even Russell shudder. "Five?"

"I see I got a lot to teach you. We've had benchwarmers among us, fornicators, deceivers, and adulterers! They acted like they were True Believers, but you see"—he held up his index finger and thumb and pinched them together—"you let the devil in this much, *this much*"—he shook his pinched fingers in Russell's face, and like he always did when he spoke of God, his face turned crimson, his eyes widened till they looked as if they'd pop from their sockets—"he'll snatch you up like that!" He snapped his fingers in the air. "Don't handle them snakes 'til you're sure you got unshakeable faith! Mighty, mighty sure!"

Russell ignored the sermon. "So, huh, you don't treat the bites?"

"It ain't my place to play God."

"You mean you don't even try to suck the venom out?"

Browning shook his head. "What kind of outfit do you think this is? We *are* The True Believers. We believe God will heal us if He sees fit. You think just maybe we should go to the doctor just in case God isn't watching?"

"I don't know." Russell sighed, looking around. They were no longer alone.

People started filtering towards the hall from different directions. Older couples arm in arm. Young couples with four, five, six children quietly padding behind. Not one was out of line, and everyone was solemn as they came together.

They sat at the long tables filled with an abundance of food; collard greens with bacon, honey ham, corn cakes and blackberry pies. Plates stacked with biscuits, potato pancakes, hogmaw, apple struddle and pickled eggs.

After prayer, Browning rose with an unexpected introduction of his nephew, welcoming him as a "new member". Caught off guard, Russell felt his face redden.

"Hallelujah!" rose from the crowd.

The plain women in their modest homemade dresses, smiled. The men, with their neatly trimmed beards that went up the sides of their faces, said, "Howdy, Brother Russell!" The children, scrubbed clean to a shine, stared.

With a nod from Browning, the congregation methodically

filled their plates. The man next to Russell, nudged him gently, handing him a plateful of a flat, round, fried vegetable. "It's the wife's fried okra. Best around," the man said.

There were sprinkles of conversation of what the Lord had done that day, followed by "amen!" and "praise the Lord!"

Russell was expecting talk of the mines, the union strikes that were sweeping the country, or the war in Korea. The war was all they talked about in prison. The young men of the congregation were of army age, yet, there they were at the table.

Browning later told Russell, "The young men of The True Believers have 'disappeared' from society, so to speak. We're in God's army, not the army of a God- forsaken government."

After supper, Russell went over to the church with everyone else, as Browning urged him to join in and witness the power of God.

Russell sat in the circle, noticing the men were separated from the women. With the help of two young boys, Browning entered the circle with the snake boxes.

"'*In like manner also*'"—he began, turning his attention on a woman in her mid-thirties wearing a bright yellow dress with large orange flowers—"'*that women adorn themselves in modest apparel, with shamefacedness and sobriety, not with broided hair, or gold, or pearls, or costly array.*' So says the scripture, Sister Georgia, in 1 Timothy 2:9. And…have you not violated the scripture?"

"Yes, Reverend," she said.

"Then why do you see fit to wear such a dress?" He threw his arms up in exasperation, then brought the palm of his hand down hard on his forehead. "Where'd you get that material, Sister Georgia, a bawdy house?"

The congregation gasped.

"The comp'ny store in Pine Mountain, Reverend."

"Sister Georgia, you tellin' me the company store only had one fabric to choose from?"

35

"No, sir."

"Then what possessed you to purchase such a high-flutin' design?"

"Satan did! Satan did!" She raised her hands to the heavens and asked God for forgiveness.

The crowd praised and prayed with her, working themselves into a frenzy.

Georgia arose and threw the dress up over her head and tossed it aside, leaving herself in just a bra and slip. Some of the congregation threw themselves on the ground, babbling incoherently.

Russell sat uncomfortably, with his palms on his knees, as the volume in the room rose. From time to time, he'd run his fingers thru his short, curly black hair.

Then he noticed her. Sitting across from him, the girl from the woods. Her eyes were closed, her hands clenched together under her chin. She wasn't babbling on like the others. She simply had her eyes closed, almost as if she were sleeping.

Suddenly she opened them and stared back at him with bewilderment, then shut them again.

With the congregation settled down, Georgia went home to change. When she returned, Browning gave a two-hour sermon on the proper attire and behavior for females. No one moved. Even the children went against nature by sitting still so long.

To confirm his revelations, he brought out the serpents, five in all, clenching them in one hand, while in the other, he held a Bible high above his head. He spoke on and on, in a series of unintelligible syllables. The crowd followed, until the volume seemed to shake the very foundation of the building.

9

Russell was a loner. Perhaps he was that way by nature, or shaped by the fact that his boyhood was a lonely one.

He spent hours alone in the woods shooting tin cans, rabbits and squirrels with his slingshot, never looked for or called in for supper. Sometimes he thought if he'd kept on walking, clear to the other side of the ridge and beyond, never stopping, no one would even notice he'd gone missing. All the while, his mother lay in bed day in and day out, depressed, chain-smoking her way through life.

Physically, he took after his father, who he never knew. Calvin Nash had hightailed it out of town while Russell was still in the womb, forming into a boy, who, along with his mother, would be banished to the far reaches of Tennessee.

It was to Franklin and Agnes' they were sent, to their hilltop squalor, high on the side of a mountain. Agnes took just enough pity on her poor sixteen-year-old sister in-law to keep Browning from sending her into the bar rooms in town to entertain the loggers.

Browning was by then well known for his corn liquor. He brought jugs of his famous "cove juice" down the rugged hillside, into the little towns in the valley, where the loggers gathered, and to the local doctors, who used it to ease pain.

While his brew was sought after, Browning himself was not well liked, for he was shrewd, and under no circumstances would do any bargaining, even if a doctor needed the liquor to relieve a patient in dire need.

When Russell was eleven, prohibition went into effect and

Browning's operation became illegal. Nevertheless, he had it in full swing.

Young Russell, doing everything he could to please his uncle, made risky runs to Knoxville in a beat-up milk truck to deliver barrels of whiskey to the speakeasies. Then he'd come home to check on his mother, who in those days had gone mad.

10

"Jolene, the gravy! Keep stirrin' or it'll burn."

It was late morning the next day. Bonnie sat at the kitchen table with her neighbor, Rita Tucker. They rarely took their eyes from their cross stitching as they spoke, except for the occasional glance Bonnie gave to her daughter, who shifted from one foot to the other in impatience at the tedious task of stirring over the hot stove.

"…and I gathered up my colorful dresses to burn in the fire," Rita said.

Bonnie replied with a sigh, "I did the same thing. Don't wanna be called out like Sister Georgia, standing in her underthings."

"And in front of the new member!" Rita shook her head. She put her work down and leaned forward into Bonnie. "And what do you make of the nephew? Looks like a rough fella to me!"

"That he do."

"And his face!"

"That's an acne problem, I think. I had a second cousin with that affliction."

"Acne or not, he's strange!"

Jolene chimed in, "Maybe he doesn't know the Lord yet."

"Mind your tongue," her mother said.

"He don't belong here, with all our virgins. Lord only knows what's on his mind," Rita replied.

Bonnie clicked her tongue and shook her head.

"Maybe he's shy, Ma."

"Jolene, what do you know about a grown man being shy?

You stay clear a that man, you hear?"

"Yes 'um."

"Take yourself to prayer."

Jolene moved away from the stove.

"Not to the prayer room. Not now. You got gravy to tend to. Do it right here, Psalms 119:176," Bonnie said.

Jolene went back to the stove and began reciting: *"'I have gone astray like a lost sheep; seek thy servant; for I do not forget thy commandments… I have gone astray like a lost sheep; seek thy servant; for I do not forget thy commandments… I have gone astray like a lost sheep; seek thy servant; for I do not forget thy commandments…'"*

Later that day, while her mother napped, Jolene put on a plain brown dress and slipped out of the house. She took in a breath of the fresh mountain air, then followed the path that threaded through the woods behind the church. Outbuildings were dotted here and there, half-hidden by ivy. Some were used for storage, one was a chicken house. One was used to keep Browning's precious rattlers.

She came upon it. Hearing a gentle clanging noise, she peered cautiously inside.

Russell, who was kneeling at the snake cage, stood up when saw her. A mouse that was in his hand jumped and scurried away. He and Jolene watched it disappear into the woods. "Guess that snake won't be eatin' today," he said to her as she backed away slightly, studying him.

Though only an inch or two taller than her, he was very imposing with his broad shoulders and thick hands. Everything about Russell was rough; his crooked fingers, his pockmarked face, the way he studied something long and hard before speaking, as if he was deciding, should he devour? Even his gray eyes seemed hard.

"Well, shoot, gotta find a mouse for that rattler." He started for the back of the outbuilding, then turned to her. "Come on."

His voice was deep and low, his speech slow and deliberate. She followed him, though not sure why. Something drew her forward, as the words of her mother and Sister Rita, spoken just hours before, replayed themselves. The more they went through her mind, the more compelling it became to follow him.

Behind the outbuilding, Russell lay on his stomach, peering into the six-inch crawl space.

"Be still," he whispered.

Suddenly as he thrust his arm out, a mouse darted past him. "Darn!"

Jolene watched the little creature scurry under twigs and leaves. She scooted after it. He joined her in the pursuit, but they soon gave up, as the mouse scuttled out of sight, into the shelter of rattlesnake ferns and decayed leaves.

Returning to the outbuilding, he again lay on his stomach, producing a little gray rodent before long. It was a baby with very large eyes.

Jolene turned away, knowing its fate.

"Come watch." Russell motioned with a nod of his head.

The girl shook her head and twisted her face. "I couldn't."

Without further prodding, he disappeared into the outbuilding, but moments later tried again to lure her in. "It's nature, is all, come on."

Pensively, she stepped inside the dank building. The snake had its mouth over the mouse's head. Methodically and ever so slightly, the snake's body slithered, so that the mouse moved further into the serpent's body.

"Ain't so awful now, is it?"

"Is the mouse still alive?" she whispered.

"No. He's suffocated."

"Oh. Did he suffer?"

"No, not one bit."

"You sure?"

"Yup."

41

"How do you know?"

"I do, is all. Shhh, watch now."

Crouched together in the semi-dark, their shoulders brushed each other lightly and Jolene became aware of it. She grew flush each time they made the slightest contact.

"It's hot in here," she said.

"It is. Let's go."

He followed her out, sizing up the girl-woman before him. Her white skin was flawless, her tall frame, boney. The dress she wore hung straight, to where he couldn't make out the curves of her body. But she was pretty. A simple, easygoing pretty. Freckles dotted her nose, giving her an almost childlike appearance and her cute little overbite had him looking again and again. But she was so young, and there he was, having spent a good part of his life behind bars.

It'd been a long time since he'd touched a female. Just sixteen when put in prison, he'd left behind the wild and brazen Caroline Woolsey. She kept him company on his bootlegging runs, drinking the brew a little too freely, and since Russell had to account for every drop, he often got smacked around for the missing liquor. He didn't care. To him, she was worth it.

Not afraid of anything, the bottle-blonde woman, eight years his senior, taught him a thing or two in the bedroom. They made a fine pair!

He knew Caroline wouldn't wait for him when he got put away. She was too unbridled, too insatiable. After just two month's, she stopped coming to see him, only to return periodically when there was a lapse of a man in her life.

The last he saw of her was in 1940. She was thirty by then, worn from boozing, cigarettes and too many men. She was no longer a shoulder for him to lean on, and Russell found himself comforting her in the miserable lot she put herself in. She was pregnant; the father of the baby had thrown her out.

Sitting across from him, red-eyed and sickly, she promised

to wait. "All I can do is wait, sweet Rusty. You's the only 'un ever cared. An' we'll pick up wheres we left off, rompin' an' funnin' like we used to, 'member?"

She glanced at her swollen belly, then looked up at him with eyes of one who hadn't enough sleep. "Oh, don't fret. I promise this thing won't be 'round when you get out. I's givin' it away. Don't care who, neither."

He just sat expressionless and stared.

"Don't want this little bastard," she said.

He'd heard that word before...so many times.

She went on, weepy-eyed, suddenly turning angry. "The fathers a lyin', cheatin' drunk, and I can't stand little brats anyhow. What we want with a brat taggin' along? Huh? You an' me, we got a whole lot of livin' to do!"

Again, he sat expressionless. The ugliness of her soul turned his stomach.

She wiped her nose with a handkerchief, sniffled, then looked up again. "I'm rentin' me a little trailer down in Shadybrook. You know, that lil' town by the tracks. The train don't bother me none. It's kinda nice to hear sometimes when I's lonely."

Caroline saw that her efforts to revive her sweet-talking Russell were failing, for he wasn't a wide-eyed boy anymore, so she leaned forward, whispering, "You always done it the best from all of 'em, you know."

For her sake, he forced a little grin. His sexual appetite was long gone, his feelings for the plundered woman before him, spent. Even she couldn't revive that in him. Not her. Not the disappointment she'd become to him.

He never saw or heard from her again. She fell into oblivion, as if she never existed. He'd lie awake at night with thoughts of their good times, mixed with an image of a tired woman, cigarette hanging from her lips, beating her unkempt child about the head.

Like the voice of an angel, Jolene brought him back from a dark place he didn't like to venture.

"I best go home," she said, turning her closed mouth up in a little smile.

"I'll walk ya up."

"No, you can't. We're not allowed to be together."

"You and me?"

"Me and anyone. Well, any male."

"Who said?"

"It's just the rules. We're putting ourselves in temptation's way."

"Just by walking together?"

She nodded. "Just by walking."

"And you believe this?"

Jolene shrugged. "I…guess. Daughters of Eve tempt men to do wicked things. That's why men need to stay close to God. And"—she added—"away from girls unless they are married."

"Daughters of Eve, huh?" he said, then decided to test her. "I don't care about the rules. Come on, let's go."

Jolene backed away. "No, really, we can't. Besides, you know, they talk about you."

"Oh yeah?"

"They say you aren't to be trusted. They think you don't really believe in God and you're hiding from something. They said—"

"Hold on there! Who's 'they'?"

"Folks, is all." She shrugged, suddenly sorry she'd said anything.

"Hell, I don't care what they say. What about you? Do you think I can be trusted?"

She looked into his gray eyes.

"I suppose. But the Reverend says non-believers are sometimes nicer than believers. They can be tricky, like a wolf in sheep's clothing or…or, a snake in the grass. We have to stay close to God to tell the difference."

Her face became hot, being studied by him the way she was.

"Can you tell the difference?" he challenged the child-woman.

"I...I think so." Her eyes searched his, as if the answer lie there in the hollow gray. "I think you're a good man."

Russell, satisfied with that, nodded. "Go on home, then, by yourself." Then added with a bit of sarcasm, "I don't want us to put ourselves in temptation's way."

Jolene walked backwards a few steps, then turned around. Her walk was clumsy, her buttocks jiggled slightly. Russell watched until she disappeared.

As she came quietly through the kitchen door, Arliss, covered in coal soot, was waiting for her.

"Where ya been, Jolene?"

"Just...just outside."

He backed her against the door. She could see the barrel of his chest heave.

"Arliss, stop!" She tried to push past him. He wouldn't budge.

He tugged at a cocklebur that clung to her dress. Then he found another, and another.

"Tsk, tsk." He shook his head. "What you doin' rollin' around in cockleburs? I outta bring you before the Elders. I really have a mind to. Line up and whip you good."

"I've done nothing wrong."

Aware of the heat from her body, so desirous of it, he leaned into her, until her breasts crushed tightly against him.

"Damn you." He gritted his teeth, holding her hips tightly in his hands, pushing against her, feeling her pelvis bone against his thigh.

With both hands she pushed him away, ran down the hall, shutting the door behind her. This time he let her go.

11

The next day Jolene helped her mother sew smock dresses. Something simple, in bleached cotton. She pinned the seams as her mother worked the machine.

"Best we stay clear of any fancy pattern," Bonnie said.

Her daughter agreed. She didn't want to be purged, half naked in front of the congregation.

Sewing was not an easy chore for Jolene. Her clumsy fingers fumbled with the pins, and she could never get the hems straight like her mother, who made it look like second nature. Frustrated, she'd want to quit, but Bonnie was patient to teach her.

"Jolene, sewing's a natural chore for a woman. Keep trying. You need to learn all these wifely things so someday you'll please your husband."

"Ma, I don't even *have* a husband yet. 'Sides, I wouldn't care if the Reverend never marries me off."

"That's foolish talk. He will, someday."

"Here." She slid the material across the table to her mother. "I've pinned the last hem. Can I go now?"

Bonnie lifted her foot from the pedal, stopping the machine and looked up. "Is this that tiresome for you?"

"Yes, Ma, yes," she said, jumping to her feet, looking out the window to the woods beyond. She turned to her mother, who watched her. "Ma…"

"What, child?"

"Nothing… I think."

She plopped down in the chair with a big sigh of a stubborn,

46

bored child and watched her mother sew a perfect hem. "Ma, can I go walking?"

"Where to?" Bonnie busied herself folding the garment.

"I don't know. I'll call on Sister Sarah and see the new baby."

"I suppose, but tuck your hair up under your bonnet when you go outdoors. I don't need another visit from Sister Agnes about your disobedience."

The girl jumped up, tucked her hair in, kissed her mothers cheek, and was out the door.

She heard her name called.

"Sister Jolene! Over here!"

Penny and Mildred waved and came to her.

"Sister Jolene." They nodded in unison.

"Sister Penny, Sister Mildred."

"We've come from Sister Sarah's."

"The babe is so sweet! It cooed the whole time we were there, and Sister Sarah is just beside herself with joy!"

"It was a joyous visit, wasn't it?" Mildred squeezed Penny's hand and smiled.

"Oh, yes, it was! Sister Jolene, are you going to see her? You really should!"

"Yes, I'm going now."

Penny said, "If we could, we'd go back with you, but we're on our way to Sister Joan's house to study. Come join us later, will you? We're going over scripture on the proper behavior of a Godly woman."

"It'll be most helpful to us all!" Mildred replied.

"I'll try and come. My mother might need me," Jolene said. Then she hurried away.

When Mildred and Penny were out of sight, she followed a path down to the creek. Russell, repairing a broken doorjamb in a nearby outbuilding, saw her. He watched as she sat on a rock by the muddy bank, removed her bonnet and untied her ponytail. Her dark hair fanned out across her back.

He set his hammer on the window ledge and went to her like it was the most natural thing in the world.

Seeing a man, she instinctively gathered her hair up in her hands.

"Don't," he said. "It's beautiful."

She smiled, letting it go.

"Ever see a jackfish in here?" he said.

"Lots of 'em. There's crawdads too. Big ones. I used to try and catch 'em when I was younger."

"I did that too when I was little. Spent whole days in the woods by myself."

"Didn't you have any friends?"

He shook his head. "Not really. We lived clear at the top of a ridge. Not a neighbor for miles."

"Where was this?"

"Buckburn, Tennessee," he said with a laugh. "God-forsaken Buckburn. It had two bars and a supply store, and one hell of a muddy road to get there."

"Why did you live in such a horrible place?"

"I lived with Franklin and Agnes. They sorta raised me."

"Oh. Where were your parents?"

"It was just my mother. We both lived there."

"Oh. Is she still in Tennessee?"

His face grew dark. "No, uh, she died a while back."

"Well, you still got family, I mean, with your Aunt and Uncle."

"Uh-huh, if that's what you want to call them," Russell said, looking off. Then he turned to her. "My Uncle's had me move in the keepers shed. Come have a look."

She shook her head. "Can't."

"Why so?"

"I told you before why."

"Who'll see us? Seems no one comes back here."

"I'm supposed to be out visiting Sister Sarah, not sitting in the woods with a man!"

"You look old enough to make your own choices."

"You don't seem to understand the way things are here, the way we live. If the Bible says something's a sin, we can't do it. We have to try to obey what God tells us."

He turned his mouth up a little. "I watch you! You don't pray all crazy like the others, hootin' and hollerin'! You sit nice and quiet like a good little church girl."

She blushed, saying nothing.

"Well, answer me this," he said. "How come pretty as you are, you ain't married by now?"

She shrugged, still blushing.

"You folks down here marry real early. I saw a girl no older than ten, carrying a baby. I said, 'That's a cute little brother you got there,' and she said it was her very own. Then, like all the other women 'round here, she ran off like I was some kind of ghost."

"Oh, that's Sister Myrna...and she's eleven."

"Eleven?"

"Yes, eleven. She had her 'episode', so she got married off. Arliss wanted her, but the Reverend said she had to marry to Lester Widdle. Arliss was mad, real mad 'cause he liked her. He came home and broke a chair! Threw it clear across the kitchen! Pa said to keep quiet about it. Then Arliss even went to the Reverend to ask for a wife, *any* wife, but the Reverend said, 'Boy, you need to take all that pent-up energy and turn it over to the Lord.' At the social, Arliss was prayed over and I think he got better after that. He's still got a mean streak in him though. Mean as ever."

"What's the 'episode'?"

"You know..." She looked at him like he was stupid, hoping he did know, because she wasn't about to explain.

He suddenly understood. Her period. She'd had her period.

By the time that young girl is twenty, she'll have had six, maybe seven kids.

So many children swarming around. So many quiet, obedient children. He wanted to move away from the subject that was beginning to unnerve him: Reverend Browning and his faithful followers.

"Let's walk a ways." He stood up, extended his hand and pulled her to her feet.

Together they forged deep into the woods, where rhododendrons were showing their last display of color and rattlesnake ferns stretched out over the woodland floor. Squirrels played overhead, jumping from limb to limb, tree to tree.

With her dress clinging around her form, Russell could make out the gentle curves of her hips. They walked in silence, to the top of a hill. On the other side, the two descended down a narrow, rutted switchback. Russell put himself in front of Jolene, and turned to help her when the path became precarious.

Her delicate hand felt warm and inviting. He held it longer than he needed, for she was soon on sure footing.

Letting go, she looked ahead to see if the way would once again become rocky, when he'd again take her hand in his calloused palms and wrap his large, misshapen fingers around hers.

Once at the bottom of the switchback, after much hand-holding and letting go, he took her face in his hands and kissed her on the mouth.

She uttered, "No," as he wrapped his arms around her and drew her to the ground.

"Just let me kiss you," he said.

Jolene turned her head, panting softly, "I'm afraid."

"I won't hurt you."

She could feel the heaviness of his body on hers. Without

thinking, or knowing why she did it, she wrapped her arms around his neck and let him kiss her.

"We shouldn't. I…I shouldn't…be here with you," she said afterward.

"But you are here with me."

"We shouldn't…"

"Okay, we won't. It's okay."

Half mad for Jolene, he felt a sense to protect her innocence. He didn't even try gentle persuasion. Couldn't do it. Not as she lay there, so trusting. Oh, she might have let him make love to her. She'd said "no" to a kiss, but then kissed him, close-lipped at first, but then passionately after. He could become her lover. Or he could love her.

He rose to his knees, helping her up. As they sat together, facing one another, he touched her hair, which hung in tendrils in the damp air. How different from Caroline she was! This was more exciting to him than the always eager, wild woman. *This* was wild; wanting, needing, but not getting, yet.

"Tomorrow, meet me at the creek," he said.

"I can't. It's Saturday. Boys'll be fishin', most likely."

Sighing, he stood, then helped her to her feet.

"Besides, if we get caught, no tellin' what'll happen."

"Well…what if I court ya proper?" Then with sarcasm, he added, "They allow that here, don't they?"

"What's courtin'?"

"Courtin"—he moved towards her, to where his lips barely touched her forehead, his voice was at a whisper—"is when a man is half crazy for a woman. He takes her for walks in the woods, they hold hands and whatnot."

"Kissing?" she whispered back.

"If she wants to."

"But we can't do that here." She turned her head slightly, so that his lips fell above her ear. He kissed it, then moved down the side of her neck.

"Anyhow, only the Reverend can put folks together."

"I'll ask him myself then."

"No, don't do that." She moved away from him, her voice rising. "You'll get me in heaps a' trouble. They'll lock me away, and you, well, they'll throw you out, most likely."

"All right, calm down. I won't say a word."

Jolene led a different way back, through hillsides thick with hemlocks and pines, stepping over rattlesnake ferns and damp moss, ascending a hill to a fire pit in a wide clearing. The pit was at least twenty feet around, contained by large rocks.

"This is where we burn things," she said, staring at the ashes of newly burned dresses.

"What things?"

She looked up into his gray eyes that grew softer each time she saw them.

"Things that matter to us. Things that make us who we are. We burn them, and then there is less of us and more of Him."

He draped his arm across her shoulder, trying to understand. "More of who?" he asked.

"Of Jesus. More of Jesus."

"What mattered to you?"

Without hesitation, she said, "My books. They're gone now and...it doesn't matter anymore. Reverend Browning took everything from us."

Russell thought of the twenty years taken from him, but left it unsaid.

Then she looked off somewhere between the cloud-draped hilltops and the sky, and her face grew dark.

"You know, I've...I've had this secret in my heart. Something so wicked. Something I shouldn't tell."

"What is it?"

"If I say it, I'll go straight to hell, I know it."

"No you won't. Tell me."

"How do you know I won't? You don't even know the least

bit of Bible, so how would you know?"

"Maybe I don't need to know the least bit of Bible. All I see in front of me is an unhappy girl, living with a bunch of crazy people with crazy ideas. So you tell me, and I promise you you'll be all right."

"I've…I've wished them all dead. Even my mother, because she never helps me. Ever!"

"What happened?"

"If I tell you, will you keep it secret? Don't let anyone know I told you."

He looked at her and nodded.

"When we first came here, I was ten. They locked me away in the prayer closet all the time, sometimes for *days*. The only way they'd let me out was if I pretended to be sorry. Sorry for what? That I wasn't joyful that they burned my books? That I couldn't go to school anymore? That…that my Pa wouldn't hold my hand anymore? Oh, it was sooo sinful to hold his hand."

"That's weird that they treated you like that."

"No, it's not. Everyone gets treated like that if the Reverend thinks they're straying from the Lord. But for me, it was all the time. *All the time!* I liked to read and had lots of books when we came here, and to him that was the biggest sin, that I liked books of the world more than the Bible. But I did love them more! I loved them, and I loved going to school, but the Reverend said 'It's bad, Jolene, very bad that you like those things!'"

Russell could do nothing but shake his head.

She went on. "Then, a few years ago, the Reverend made this man, Brother Walter Blair, handle the snakes, because he said Brother Walter was backsliding from the Lord. Brother Walter loved to fish, and I guess he loved it a little too much! The Reverend said Brother Walter loved fishing more than he loved God and Brother Walter said, 'That's not true, I love the

Lord with all my heart.' And the Reverend said, 'If you love the Lord with all your heart you should handle the snakes.' And Brother Walter said, 'Okay, I will, because I know how much I love the Lord and how dare you question it!' We even thought there'd be a fistfight, they shouted so bad! And for him to speak to the Reverend like that was unspeakable! Secretly, I was glad he did! So, we gathered around, and the Reverend handed him the snakes one by one. They didn't do anything at first, just hissed a little and shook their rattlers. We were all relieved, and started to praise the Lord. Then suddenly, a snake darted at Brother Walter's face, biting him in the cheek. He turned pale and fell on the floor. We anointed him with oil right then and there and prayed all night, but he died the next day. The Reverend said he knew Brother Walter had strayed and there was the proof right in front of us and we'd all better live as close to the Gospel as possible so the same thing doesn't happen to us!"

"Man, that's nuts!"

"No, it's not. It's true. And you want to know something else? Every time I lie about my repentances, the Reverend knows. He'll even know that I let you kiss me."

"No, he won't find out about that. Don't worry."

Jolene sighed. "Oh, he will. He knows everything. *Everything.*"

12

Franklin Browning leaned on the threshold of the keeper's shed door for a long time before he said anything. Russell was sitting on the floor, knees drawn up and spread, as he whittled a stick of hickory. It had taken the shape of a cowboy, hat tipped over his eyes, as if he were sleeping.

"Where'd you learn to whittle like that?"

"Where you think?"

Franklin turned to the windowsill, where several wooden figurines stood. Cowboys, horses, a cougar charging. All impressive, to the last detail.

Browning held one in his hands and said, "'*Thou shall not make unto thee any graven image, or any likeness of anything that is in Heaven above or that is in the earth beneath.*'"

Russell glanced up for a moment, stopping short of rolling his eyes.

"'*Thou shall not bow thyself to them, nor serve them, for I the Lord thy God am a jealous God.*'"

Russell put down the blade and wood, then rested his palms on his knees, looking up at Browning.

"Now, what does *that* have to do with me?" he said.

"Don't care for our way of life, do you, boy?"

"The jury's still out, but so far I think you're a little nuts."

"That's a mighty harsh accusation coming from an ex-con. Folks are talkin', asking why I allow the heathen to live amongst us. Can't even win over my own kin."

Russell stood and brushed the shavings from his trousers. He walked outside into the gray afternoon and dug his hands deep into his pockets.

Browning could roll God's word off his tongue to condemn any infraction on the part of his congregation. It was like a sledgehammer that weighed down on them all, and already, after being there for less than two weeks, Russell was feeling that weight. Only he didn't let it crush him. "So, it's all about your image! Makes you look bad."

"It's not about me looking bad. It's about you dwelling with a body of believers. Bottom line is, if you're not a believer, you can't stay. We are one body here, *one body*."

Browning emphasized his point by intertwining his fingers together tightly, and if it weren't for that freckled-nosed young woman who literally came tumbling into his life, Russell would have gathered his few belongings and marched right out of there. Maybe he'd have even wiped the stupid grin from his uncle's face.

Instead, he changed his tone, thinking only of Jolene. He needed to see her again. "Okay," he said. "I understand. Look, just give me some time to think about it."

Then Browning resounded sternly, "*'Wide is the gate, and broad is the way that leadeth to destruction, and many there be which go in thereat, but strait is the gate, and narrow is the way which leadeth unto life, and few there be that find it.'* Son, I pray you choose the proper gate."

13

It was huckleberry season. Time for huckleberry pies and jams. The women and girls made their way through the woods to gather them. This time, they had on their smock dresses. Some were pale blue, some bleached white. Some were brown. But they all possessed the simplicity that would not set one woman apart from the other. All eyes faced forward, all mouths recited the psalm dictated by Agnes Browning.

The women were not alone as they entered the clearing. Russell was at the edge of the tree line, sawing a downed hickory into workable pieces for his carvings. The gentle female chantings he heard in the distance stopped.

Agnes barked, "Stick to your bush, Sisters!"

Jolene went red in the face when she saw Russell, watching from the corner of her eye as Agnes went to him and said something that had him gathering his things in his arms and heading into the thicket, out of sight. Jolene watched every part of him disappear.

Penny, who was to Jolene's left, said, "I'm glad he's gone."

"Me too." Sarah Harrington was to her right, her cooing baby strapped to her back.

Jolene listened, quietly.

"I heard he carves idols. He may even be a devil-worshipper. Sister Sarah, we should pray over the baby, since he was so close to us," Penny said.

"Lord," Sarah said, "protect my little Jonah from the snare of the devil and from any evil this stranger has brought to our humble community, I pray, Amen."

"Amen," Penny said.

Sarah said, "I don't mean to speak unkindly of another, but he does give me the willies."

"I don't know why they don't just send him away. I heard my pa say, and I heard it accidentally, of course, that Brother Russell was after the virgins. He told me not to look him in the eye, or he might cast a spell on me and lure me away," Penny commented, then added, "Sister Jolene, what's wrong? Your face is red as a beet!"

Agnes Browning approached at that moment. "Are you girls praising the Lord, or chatting needlessly?"

"Sister Agnes," they all said, nodding their heads.

"Sister Jolene looks a bit…a bit flush in the face," Penny said.

Jolene went on picking huckleberries like she'd never picked them before, ignoring the attention brought to her.

"What's wrong, Sister Jolene? If you're feelin' poorly, why haven't you asked for prayer?"

Jolene straightened up, took a deep breath, and looked Agnes square in the eyes and said, "Sister Agnes, I'm not feeling poorly at all."

"I'm glad to hear that, Sister Jolene, now why don't you girls recite the first chapter of John aloud the rest of the day, and stop your silly, worldly shenanigans."

"'*In the beginning was the Word, and the Word was with God, and the Word was God…all things were made by Him, and without him was not anything made that was…*'"

Penny leaned close to Jolene. "You were flush!…'*in Him was light…*'"

"I'm fine!"

"'*…and the light was the light of man…*' you fibbed, didn't you, Sister Jolene?"

"Sister Penny, I'm trying to recite Gods word, so please, leave me alone!…'*there was a man sent from God.*'"

14

She knew she had to go to him. The rain was coming down hard, and by the time she'd reached the keeper's shed, she was soaked and out of breath.

He was there, carving in the light of a kerosene lamp, the rain tip-tapping from the leaves of the trees onto the tin roof. He answered the gentle knock, pulled her in from the rain and took her in his arms. Then he drew her to his bed, and without a word between them, he made love to her.

After, she lay against his chest, her soft breathing warm on his skin. She reached up, touching his face, her fingers running over the rough surface of his skin.

It had stopped raining. The sun came out, spreading light through the dark corners of the shed.

"You okay?" he whispered.

She nodded.

He drew her chin up.

"You sure?"

"He'll know."

"Who? Uncle Frank? No he won't! Don't be silly."

"He knows everything."

"He doesn't know everything. You're afraid of him, is all."

Jolene lay there with Franklin Browning's face so clear in her mind, with his hard eyes and stern expression set firm on his face.

"You get out from under this place, and you'll see I'm right."

"Then why don't the snakes bite him? Tell me that."

"I don't know. I only know I'm leaving before long. I got to. This place is weird."

"Why'd you come up here then? Didn't you know your uncle was famous?"

"Famous, hell!" He let out a laugh, nudging her up against him. "He's not famous, sugar! Just a crazy ole' man! He likes power, that's all. He's got all you folks worshipping him. I know he's lovin' it."

"So you don't think he hears from God?"

"No, I don't. I think he'll say and do anything to get people to think he's important. Maybe he does believe he hears from God. I don't know which is worse, but I know it's hogwash, all of it."

This was something new to think about, that maybe the Snakeman was a fake, but the thought that her whole way of life, the way of life at The True Believers Holiness Church, her struggle to walk upright with the Lord and spending her days feeling like she was missing the mark somehow, but not sure why, was a lot to swallow. And what about Brother Walter?

"I'm leaving here," he said, "and you'll go with me. Jolene"—he pulled her chin up—"go with me."

She turned her face and pulled away, sitting up, covering her nakedness with the blanket.

"Don't ask me that now," she said, slipping her legs through her dress. "I sinned with you…a sin…a sin that could have me struck down!"

She stood, moving away from his hand that reached for her.

"Don't. I'm confused," she said, wiping tears that pooled in the corner of her eyes.

She went to the window, noticing the sun had crept to the corner of the sky. She'd be looked for. As Jolene turned, she knocked over two of the wooden figures that sat on the sill.

"Oh! I'm so sorry!" She picked them up and set them back in their places. He sat on the edge of the bed, watching her.

"I…I need to go. They'll be looking for me."
She left in haste, without another word.

15

As he put the blade to wood, the walnut limb took the shape of a wild horse. Reared up, nostrils flared, its mane flowed back as if tossed by a surging motion. Each movement from his hands were driven by his heart and the life he brought to the wood was the life she'd brought to him.

He stopped to wipe tears that ran down his face and shuttered at this strange emotion that gripped his heart.

That chunk of wood, that piece of his soul.

His wild horse. His hazel-eyed Jolene.

He whittled until his eyes hurt under the strain of the dim light, then he went to sleep.

16

She had left for home too late. The pieces of sky through the trees had turned pink, the hollow already darkened. She ran through the damp woods, into the open air of the pines and in through the kitchen door, where her mother was bent over the oven.

She straightened up when she heard the door open. "Jolene, where have you been? And what happened to your head covering?"

Jolene reached up feeling her bare head. She'd forgotten it.

George appeared in the doorway, fresh from the shower. When he saw his daughter standing there, his face grew stern. "You weren't at Sarah's. We sent Buddy to fetch you," he said.

The girl was bombarded with questions she answered with lies, for the truth would surely have her brought before the congregation and worse.

The missing prayer bonnet, the disheveled hair, her long absence was explained away with a wild tale that she'd seen a bear, ran from it, and then was lost in the deepest part of the hollow.

"You know these woods better n' anybody," Arliss said. "You're lying."

By this time, she was sitting in a chair in the kitchen, surrounded by folded arms and skeptical faces. George was quiet, listening, shaking his head, finally resolving that bear or no bear, she'd taken her mind off the Lord to have come home in such a state. To the prayer closet it was, and she went without resistance into the darkness, knowing her father was probably on his way to fetch the Reverend to report, once again, the errant ways of his daughter.

With the wetness of her lover still between her legs, with aching thighs where his weight bore down, she sat in darkness. Her mind drifted from Russell's hand exploring the surface of her skin, to the wrath of her family. Was the Reverend marching across the compound to throw open the door and drag her by the arm to the cold floor of the church? By the power of God, he would know her sin. By her lover's scent he would know she lusted after the flesh.

"I never asked to be a daughter of Eve!" she said aloud.

"'And the Lord God said, Behold, the man has become as one of us, to know good and evil, and therefore the Lord God sent him forth from the garden of Eden...'"

17

George Mosley didn't march over to the Reverend, deciding to leave it until morning. The family had supper and went to bed, leaving Jolene in the darkness, without food or water.

That night, Browning had a revelation in the form of a dream.

There was a baby in a womb, floating in the water sack, sucking its thumb. It revealed itself to be a boy, and on his head, a crown of thorns. His delicate palms bore the markings of nails, and blood dripped from them, mingled with the water that surrounded him.

"*And she brought forth a man child, who was to rule all nations with a rod of iron: and her child was caught up unto God, and to his throne...*"

In the dream, Browning saw the swollen belly of the mother, and then the mother herself.

Just a shadow at first, she drifted towards him, coming into focus, revealing herself.

Jolene Mosley, large with child, bathed in white light, smiled. Jolene Mosley, looking like an angel, reached for him.

18

She woke, disoriented, hungry, thirsty, needing to relieve herself. She listened for sounds outside the room, and for a while, there were none. Then she heard the rattles of the serpents, then "hallelujah" and "praise the Lord!" from somewhere in the house. People were there, lots of them.

Pressing her ear to the door, she heard pieces of words:"…a woman clothed in the sun…under her feet…with child…to be delivered…."

Voices rose and fell as she strained to hear.

"…brought forth…child…rod of iron…."

Jolene moved away from the door. She could no longer hear Browning's words, for the noise level of prayer was earsplitting. Where was that passage he was reciting? Where? Where? And what did it mean? It was somewhere in Revelations, but she couldn't recall it fully, only knowing it was about the latter days.

"Why are they holding prayer in my house? Surely they've discovered my sin of fornication," she thought.

It grew quiet. She heard the turning of the key. The door was opened. Browning stood there, candle in hand. He entered the room, then closed himself in.

Jolene cowered to the corner of the room, waiting to be cast before the congregation, waiting for the cane, reproach, waiting to have the serpents thrust at her, so great was her sin. There'd been others who'd sinned as she had, and they were dead from snakebite, buried in the swamps of the hollow, far from glory, where Satan will claim them in fiery chains when Jesus returns.

Browning spoke softly, the flickering candle casting shadows on his face. "'*Behold the handmaiden of the Lord.*'"

The girl, dizzy from hunger, pressed her back against the wall as Browning bent down, placing his hands on her forehead. He was in a trance-like state.

"'*Blessed art thou among women, and blessed is the fruit of thy womb.*'"

Jolene trembled at the prophecy, wondering why she wasn't cast out, like Adam and Eve in the Garden of Eden. Instead, Browning was kneeling at her feet, kissing her palm.

"'*For He hath regarded the low estate of his handmaiden: for behold, from henceforth all generations shall be blessed.*'"

He stood up over her saying, "We will come fetch you shortly."

"I don't understand," she said.

"You carry the seed of the Endtime Prophet."

Still not having her wits about her, she looked up at him and uttered a weak, "No."

He smiled his half smile. "It's a wonderful thing, my child, to be chosen to carry this special baby. Now I know why Satan fought so hard to keep you from walking the straight and narrow."

"No!" she cried. "No! What are you talking about?"

He held the crown of her head in his hands, trying to sooth her. "Lord, help Sister Jolene to understand. Help her not to be afraid for this beautiful thing You have done. Help her to accept her mission, for You said, '*Let us not be weary in well doing; for in due season, ye shall reap, if ye faint not.*' Shhh, now be still. We are preparing a place for you, and then we will bring you there."

"Reverend…"

"Child?" he said.

She looked into his eyes. The startling blue, the stern, yet handsome face. A face she'd feared since she first saw it. A face that now looked on her tenderly.

Russell had been wrong. The Reverend knew everything.

"I'll wait," she said.

19

Russell rose before sunrise, spent the morning exploring the hollows on the furthest ridge. He did some fishing, whittling, staying clear of the True Believers. Later that day, when his uncle came down the path for the snakes, he stayed out of sight. All afternoon he heard the prayer meeting. It went on for hours. He knew nothing of the frenzy that was going on due to Browning's recent prophecy.

It'd been four days since he'd seen her, four long days since he held her and asked her to leave with him. Hopes that she would come running down the path faded with each passing day. He decided to wait just two more days. It was Wednesday night. By Saturday morning, he'd be gone.

As Friday rolled around, he carefully wrapped his wooden figures in his spare shirt, to tuck away for the journey. Then he went outside to go fishing one last time at the creek. That's when he discovered Jolene's prayer bonnet crumpled just outside his door. The delicate white lace was wet and muddy. He picked it up and looked at it for a long time. He'd take it with him, to remember.

Arliss startled him.

"That's my sister's, ain't it?"

"I don't know."

"Well, I know it is!" He snatched it from Russell's hand.

Russell moved his chest forward into Arliss, to where they were barely touching. "You little punk!"

"I ain't no punk! I'm lookin' out for my sister is what I'm doin'. What're you doin' with her bonnet?"

"I *found* it, just now, you dumbass."

Each waited for the other to throw the first punch, but they both held back. Arliss was jumpy, his fist balled up.

"I *know* she came back here. I saw 'er. What were you doin' with her, huh? You touch her? Huh?"

It took every ounce of discipline on Russell's part not to hit him and not to betray Jolene. "Mind your own damn business."

"She *is* my business, and she don't want nothin' to do with you no more. She's a True Believer, not a heathen like you."

"Take the bonnet and get outta my face, boy."

Arliss took a step back and said with his cocky grin, "Oh, I will. And I'll make certain she gets it!"

20

Jolene leaned her head over the washbowl while her mother poured warm water over her freshly shampooed hair. Later, they sat on the porch to escape the mugginess of the house, where Bonnie brushed the girl's hair, wound it tightly in a bun, and helped her with her bonnet.

Jolene thought of her other bonnet, lying somewhere in the keeper's shed.

That rainy day in Russell's shed came to her again and again. She found herself longing for his touch, longing for the understanding she had never known until she met him. She found herself missing him terribly.

What if the baby growing in her belly was Russell's child? What about the prophecy? How would the Reverend have known without a revelation from God? Jolene's mind was clouded with confusion.

The True Believers Holiness Church, her community, her brethren, people she'd lived amongst, been condemned by again and again, seemed to love her now. They prayed over her throughout the day. She kneeled in humility, begging God to help her see the truth, that she was indeed a chosen woman.

They'd prepared a small cottage for her, transforming the potter's shed behind the church into a nesting place. Browning appointed handmaidens to tend to her every need and on Friday, the day of her coronation to honor her new status amongst the Church, she sat, hands folded neatly on her lap, in the middle of the room. They came, one by one, from the eldest to the youngest, to honor her, kissing her hand.

Each anointed her head with oil and repeating, "'*Thou art blessed amongst women.*'"

Her mind was elsewhere, at the bottom of the switchback where Russell first kissed her, then it drifted to his hands removing her wet clothes, holding her, telling her that if she left the True Believers she'd see…

"Jolene, the last of them have gone," her mother said. "You should get some rest. I'll bring you a plate of supper in an hour or so."

She kissed her daughter's forehead and lifted her chin. "Don't look so glum, child."

"Ma…this just can't be!"

"Jolene."

"Ma, it doesn't feel right. I just don't—"

"Hush, Jolene. I've always known you were a good girl. I always knew something good was to come of you. You are the chosen woman. It's a humbling mission, but I know you can do it, with God's help. It just all comes to light, why you've been so troublesome. You should be happy now that it's all clear."

"But Ma, it's not clear, not to me! Please, listen."

"What is it? Do you want me to get the Reverend? He'll help you."

"No, I just want—"

The girl stopped herself. Why would things be different now, when all her life no one understood?

She let her mother leave her, but she was not alone long. As she put her head in her hands to cry, she heard Arliss.

"Look what I found." He stood at the door, sneering, holding her missing prayer bonnet. "Guess where I found it?"

She shook her head weakly. "I don't know and I don't care."

He laughed. "You know exactly where I found it!"

He threw it at her. "Immaculate conception! Ha! You're a whore is what you are! If I thought anyon'd believe me, I'd tell, but the Reverend really thinks you're some holy chosen woman! You know, they're going to take that baby from you."

"I don't believe you. Go away, Arliss." Jolene didn't raise her voice or get upset. She just sat there, staring at the floor, where the muddied bonnet lay.

"Oh, yes they are! The Reverend and Sister Agnes are raising that baby. They said so."

"It's not true."

"It is true," he said.

He took her face in his hands, pulling it up. She didn't try to wrestle away from his grip, but she refused to look at him.

"Look at me! Look at me!" He shook her. "Okay, don't then." He put his lips on hers, pushing her face against his, trying to force his tongue through her clenched teeth. He tore her bonnet from her head, tugging at her tightly wrapped bun. Hairpins fell to the floor. Still, she didn't struggle against him.

The chair tipped backwards, sending her down. She lay there, on her back, her long hair tangled around her. Arliss unbuttoned his pants. Jolene didn't move. Not a muscle. She didn't pull down her dress that was exposing her thighs. She didn't close her legs together or cry out for help. All she saw was Russell's face. How far away had he gone? It didn't matter now.

She looked Arliss in the eyes when he got on his knees, placing himself between her legs. "Why?" she said.

He was shaking as he reached inside his pants. "Shut up! Shut up!"

Just then, they heard Buddy, calling close by, "Arliss!"

Arliss quickly stood up, scrambling to button his pants, but Jolene didn't move. He pushed her leg against the other one, closing them.

Buddy came in saying, "Arliss, Pa's lookin' for you." He turned to Jolene. "What happened to you?"

"Buddy! Tell Jolene what they're gonna do with her baby. Who's gonna raise it? Go ahead. Tell her! She doesn't believe me." He wiped the sweat from his face.

Buddy shrugged his shoulders. "The Reverend is going to raise it, to lead the world to the Endtime. What's the big deal?"

"Tell her the rest of the prophecy."

"She doesn't know?"

"No, I don't know! What is it?" She jumped to her feet, grabbing Buddy at the shoulders. "Tell me! Tell me!"

"Okay! Okay! Let go! I'll tell you! The Reverend said, 'She shall travail much and lose her life bringing forth the chosen one.'"

"What?"

"'...and the chosen one shall be raised by the community in the ways of the Lord.'"

"Where is that in the Bible?" she cried. "Where? Tell me!"

Arliss sneered, but Buddy shook his head. "I don't know. The Reverend said it. Jolene what's wrong with you?"

Jolene bolted past them, into the woods, half-running towards the keeper's shed.

"He's gone! Your lovers left you!" Arliss cried after her.

She didn't go in once she reached the shed. She'd seen all she needed to see; the wooden figures were gone from the windowsill. When she turned, Arliss had her trapped against the door. Buddy was soon at his side.

"Why're you crying?" Arliss said. "It *is* true, isn't it, you and him? I knew it!"

"Who?" Buddy said.

"Russell. Jolene and Russell. That's no immaculate conception, little brother! That's a bonified bastard she's carrying!"

Buddy's face soured. He looked at his sister. "Is it true?"

"Oh, it's true, ain't it, *Sister Jolene*? Buddy, I'm takin' her inside here. You stay on the lookout if anyone comes."

"What for?"

"You know. She must be good at fucking, all the practice

she'd had with that criminal. He's a murderer Jolene! A murderer!"

Jolene stood there, back against the door, eyes closed, hoping for once that Buddy would be on her side. "No, Arliss." He shook his head. "That ain't right. Let 'er go."

"Come on, Buddy. You tellin' me you never thought about it?"

"Let 'er go. It ain't right to do that, and you know it!"

"But she's a whore. I got proof!"

"Let me go," she cried. "You're not without sin! In fact, you're worse, because you're such a hypocrite! Well, I'm telling them everything! All the awful things you've done to me in secret! Everything!"

"I could care less," he said. "Go on! They won't believe you!"

He moved aside. The girl ran down the path, disappearing into the snake shed. Crouching down, Jolene, suddenly calm and resolute, unlatched the cage of the largest rattler. It coiled in the corner, rattler shaking wildly. She reached inside. The serpent drew its head back, and in an instant, dug its fangs between her thumb and forefinger on her right hand, then drew its head back, recoiling, hissing. The young woman never flinched.

Up on her feet, she held the injured hand at the wrist. There was little blood, just two deep puncture wounds. She turned. Her brothers stood at the door, looked at her hand, then up, into her dull eyes.

"You didn't," Arliss uttered. "Holy God!"

Jolene swayed on her feet as the venom raced through her blood, opened her mouth as if to speak, but nothing came. Her eyes rolled to the back of her head and she collapsed on the dirt floor.

21

They came from all directions, converging on the Mosley porch, wanting to know why, wanting to know what happened.

As the True Believers gathered, Arliss looked around for Russell. He told Buddy to help if they spotted him, to force Russell out before the community and make him confess that he lay with Jolene, but Russell had yet to appear.

A vigil was held over the fevered girl, her head was anointed with oil. Browning was certain she'd be healed, carrying the Holy child, as she was, but as her temperature rose, Bonnie grew alarmed.

At ten p.m., the entire congregation, save for Bonnie, who remained at her daughter's side, withdrew to hold a prayer meeting in church.

Arliss didn't want to go. He wanted to keep an eye out for Russell and keep him away from Jolene.

"Pa," he said, "let me stay and help Ma with Jolene. She might need me."

"We need your prayers more, Son." He threw his arms over his son's shoulders and walked him to the church. "I'm glad you're so concerned for her well-being, but prayer is the best thing you can do for her."

Agnes lingered behind. She rung out a washcloth and handed it to Bonnie.

"Keep her forehead cool," she said to Bonnie, who'd already been caring for Jolene for hours. "I know she's your daughter, but now, she belongs to all of us. Now that God has given her a great mission, you mustn't let your emotions overtake you.

I'm going to the hall to pray, but you need to stop crying. It shows your lack of faith that God has a mission for her. If you can't stop, then you go pray and I will stay with her."

Bonnie sucked in air and swallowed hard. "I'm okay. I do believe God can heal her. Go pray with the others."

Agnes didn't look convinced. "I'll go, and later, I'll check on you."

Bonnie was relieved to be left alone. Why would Jolene do such a thing as to handle the rattlers? She just couldn't figure it out, and even as she tried to leave it to prayer and give it over to God, something tugged at her heart.

The mother wept, in spite of what Agnes said. She wiped Jolene's forehead, whispering scripture to her daughter, who tossed in delirium.

Suddenly Jolene shot up out of bed. "Mama!" She looked past her mother with glazed eyes, trembling uncontrollably.

The outburst caused Bonnie to cry harder. She'd heard about this, people getting a sudden burst of energy just before they die. The "death walk" they called it.

"God, don't take her from me!" she wailed.

She tried to get Jolene to lie down, but the girl seemed to have somewhere to go.

"Mama," she said again. "Tell Russell to wait. Tell him! Mama!" She grabbed her mother's arm with such force.

"I will," she said.

"Please. Mama, please tell him."

Jolene lay down with her mother's guiding hand, repeating Russell's name in delirium.

"Mama…"

"Yes, Jolene."

"Russell."

The whites of her eyes showed, then she closed her eyes.

22

Bonnie knocked frantically on the keeper's shed door.

Russell's habits in prison had him wide-awake in a split second.

It was a woman calling softly, "Brother Russell! Brother Russell, please wake up!"

When he opened the door, Bonnie could barely say the words. "It's Jolene! Please...please come...she's been bit by a rattler!"

The story of Brother Walter was the first thing that came to mind.

"What? Did that son-of-a-bitch make her handle the snakes?"

"No! No! Come! Quick!"

He was already racing ahead of her, to the house and through the back door. Bonnie looked around. She was certain no one had seen them, and in the church building she could hear voices rising and falling in prayer. She turned inside, finding Russell at Jolene's bedside, holding her hand. The girl's breathing was short and difficult, her skin red from fever.

"Oh, shit," Russell said, looking at the puncture wounds on Jolene's hand. "When did it happen?"

"Just before dark. Five o'clock, maybe."

"Five o'clock! What's the matter with you people? It's too late. The poisons in her veins."

"Everyone's at the church praying for her."

He spoke through his clenched teeth. "They're over there *praying*?"

Bonnie touched his arm. "She's been crying for you. I don't know why."

"Because I love her, that's why. Mrs. Mosley, I need to take her away or she'll die."

"But they're praying for her now."

"Like they prayed for Walter Blair?"

"Walter Blair? What do you know of Walter Blair? Brother Russell, God *does* heal, according to our faith."

"Tell me then, do you have the faith she'll be healed?"

"I don't know," she confessed.

"How did she get hold of the snakes if Franklin didn't give them to her?"

"She...she went there on her own, to the cages, and...she took them out."

"Mrs. Mosley." Russell grabbed Bonnie by the shoulders, a little rougher than he intended. "Open your eyes! Your daughter wants *out*!"

"Out?"

"Out of here! Out of this!"

Locked in his grip, she cried, "What about the baby?"

"What baby?" he shouted.

"The baby growing inside her!"

"How do you know there's a baby?" He shook her, knowing she was frightened, but he couldn't help himself, and he knew at any moment she might cry out for help.

"The Reverend had a prophecy that she was carrying a baby—"

Russell let Bonnie go and scooped Jolene up in his arms. "Mrs. Mosley, look me in the eye and tell me you love your daughter."

"I do! You know I do," she cried.

"Then get out of my way!"

She followed him down the hall to the front door.

"Wait! Please!" She disappeared into the back of the house,

returning, handing Russell a key. "It's to the car."

He looked down at the little mother, and for a moment their eyes met with understanding.

She followed him, opened the car door, where he placed Jolene gently down in the backseat.

Bonnie looked around nervously. "Push it down the hill before you start it. If they hear you, they'll come after you, and the law around here won't help. You're on your own. And please, give her this"—she handed him a small package wrapped in brown paper.

Russell squeezed Bonnie's hand as she wept. Then he pushed the car down the hill as she had asked. He glanced in the rearview mirror, where she stood wringing her hands, until she disappeared in the dark.

23

At 112 West Street, Jolene sat in a dimly lit room, staring blankly out the window.

A bed was in the corner, a dresser beside it and nothing else, except the chair she sat upon.

Overhead, pipes ran along the length of the high ceiling, knocking and hissing when the boiler kicked on.

Once in a while, rubber soles squeaked on tile as someone made their way down the hall.

Peeled paint, baby blue, spotted the walls, exposing the whitewash underneath.

There she sat, looking past the deserted alley, into the brick building beyond, where students were finishing up the day's classes.

Her mind was elsewhere, somewhere between the deep hollows of Kentucky and the lonely road that brought her to the strangeness of the city.

Scenes with Russell replayed in her mind. Words spoken. The way he touched her. Had she missed something? If a man wants you and is tender, he must love you, right?

"Jolene, may I come in?"

Jolene nodded to Patricia, the papist woman who was about the same age as Bonnie, but without the telltale lines of a hard-boiled life.

The nun sat herself on the bed.

"Have you thought about things? You know, what we talked about yesterday?"

"I don't need to think about it. I'm not changing my mind."

She never took her eyes from the blonde-haired student across the alley, chewing her pencil, then tapping it on the desk.

"Jolene, you need to think of what's best for the baby."

The school bell rang. The students gathered their books together.

"I have. It needs to be with me. I'm its mother."

"But it won't have a father. A child needs a father and a mother to thrive properly."

"You'd rather that strangers raise my baby?"

"People who adopt babies love them as if they were their own."

The students gathered and talked about what they would do that night. On Fridays, it seemed the whole town went to the movies. All except the residents of 112 West Street.

"And what will happen to me? I'm supposed to just go away and pretend it never happened?"

Patricia didn't answer right away, then she said, "Well, yes. You'll go on with your life and have more children after you're married. Listen, you still have four months to decide."

It sounded flat and cold, even to her.

"I know all the others are giving theirs up, and I know you think I *should,* but you can ask me a million times, but I'm not changing my mind."

Patricia sighing, said, "What will you say to your baby when his tummy is empty and you have no food, or he says 'Mommy, my feet hurt,' because his shoes are too small for his feet?...or, 'where's my father?'"

Jolene turned around. "That's a cruel thing to say. Have *you* ever had a child growing in your belly?"

"Why, no. Of course not."

"Exactly! And that's why you and the others shouldn't be telling us we can't or shouldn't be mothers to our babies. So what if the world frowns on our bastard children? We'll love them." She pushed back tears. "If I have to strap that baby on my back and pick cotton to feed it and buy it shoes, I will! But no one's going to rip this baby from me!"

Jolene turned her angry face away from the nun who'd shown her so much kindness, but she couldn't say she was sorry.

The light in the school had gone out.

"What about school? Jolene, please."

Jolene was silent as the pipes played their symphony and the students poured into the alley below.

Finally, she said, in a whisper, "Tell me again, about the time you saw him."

Patricia groaned. "Oh, Jolene, again?"

"Please, tell me. Tell me everything."

"Okay. The hospital called me in. They said they had a girl in the ward, a pregnant girl, gravely ill from snakebite. They said there was a man with you, but he was not your husband. They thought I should come and check on you, because the man was vague and wouldn't tell them where you had come from or who your family was. So I went.

"He was at your bedside. You were still very sick. I talked with him a bit and asked him very kindly if he was the father of your child, to which he wouldn't answer. I asked him what he planned to do once you recovered. 'Does she have a family you could take her home to?' I asked. He said, 'No, and I don't know what to do. I don't have a place to start.' That's what he said, 'I don't have a place to start.' I didn't know what he meant, but I could tell he didn't want to speak to me, or anyone else. He seemed very…out of place.

"A week later, the hospital called me to tell me that Russell had asked me to come see him, which I did. He was waiting for me downstairs and he looked terrible, like he hadn't slept. He handed me ten dollars. He said it was all he had, and asked me to promise to use it to buy you shoes and some clothes, because you'd come away with nothing. Of course, I promised. Then he made me promise to take good care of you and not to send you home. He was very strong on the subject. 'Whatever you do,' he said, 'don't send her home.' Then…he left."

"And he was crying."

"Yes, and he was crying."

24

Gloria, Celia and Valerie talked about the fathers of their babies after mass one Sunday. They were sitting in the common room. Jolene rarely joined in the chatter, for she had nothing in common with girls who would someday go home. Girls who should be cooking supper for their husbands, polishing the furniture, mending clothes. Picking names for the baby.

"I didn't even know him that well," Gloria said. "He was my best friend's cousin visiting from Florida. It wasn't my first time, you know. I've done it lots and lots of times, but I know this one's his."

"Mine…" Celia began, "he was my boyfriend. He talked me into it, but I didn't want to."

"Then why did you?" Valerie said.

"Because he said we should. 'It'll mean we love each other.' But when I told him about the baby, he said he didn't want me."

"Don't cry." Valerie hugged her. "The very same thing happened to me. Donny said he loved me and then when I told him, he disappeared. He denied everything. Now he's finishing school, living his life just like before and I'm…here."

"Jolene," Gloria said. "Jolene, stop reading! I know you're listening. Tell us about your bad boy."

The girl ignored her.

"Come on! You *never* tell us *anything* and it's driving us nuts! It's driving me nuts anyway!"

"I've nothing to tell." She turned a page and continued reading.

"You're pregnant! How could you not have anything to tell?"

She kept her eyes on the book and said, "He wasn't a bad boy."

"Well, he didn't marry you. You're here. Alone. Tell me he was a choir boy, will you!"

"But he isn't bad."

"Oh, then what do you call him, a saint?" Gloria replied.

"He saved my life."

"You don't make any sense! None at all!" Gloria said.

"Yeah," Valerie replied. "What's that supposed to mean?"

"She means from the snakebite. But still, he left you," Celia said.

Jolene closed her book and stood up to go. "It means I'm free to discover myself. He did save my life."

25

They sat on wooden crates, legs spread, arms reaching as far down as their swollen bellies would allow.

The four girls were in the basement, washing laundry in large metal tubs. When they were finished, they would hang the clothes and linens in the boiler room.

"The ladies from the agency visited me yesterday," Gloria said. "They seemed real nice. They'll come to the hospital, and they said if I want to hold the baby for a little while, I can."

"I wouldn't want to," Valerie said.

Gloria asked, "You wouldn't be the least bit curious? Well, I would. I'd want to know what it looked like."

Valerie said, "Please, I don't want to talk about it."

"Jolene is keeping hers," said Celia, glancing at the girl to see her reaction. She secretly admired Jolene, but didn't dare befriend her, because she was considered odd.

"How are you gonna go home with a baby, Jolene? Don't you know what your town will make of you? Gosh, it was hard enough for my mother to come up with a story about me being gone. Just a heck of a time! 'Where's *Gloria*?' 'When's *Gloria* coming home?' 'Why hasn't *Gloria* come home for Easter?' It's just so hard for people to mind their own business. Can't a girl just live her life? So what will you do, Jolene, walk around town with your head hanging low?"

Jolene was wringing out bed linens, and without lifting her eyes said, "*It is* just so hard for people to mind their own business."

"I'm telling you, I know! Just better you give it up and go on like nothing happened," Gloria said, "because no decent man will want to marry you when it's so obvious what you've done. My mother said it's best to just come home empty-handed and find a decent man. It'll be the biggest secret I ever had to keep, but I'm good at keeping my mouth shut, really."

"Yes, I'm sure you are," Jolene replied.

Celia asked, "So your parents said you could bring the baby home? How lucky for you, I think."

"Bad advice is more like it!" Gloria said.

Jolene didn't respond.

"You'll ruin your future," Gloria said.

"I think we should leave her alone," Valerie said. "We'll all be crying when we give ours up, so maybe what she's doing isn't so bad."

"Don't bother, Valerie," Jolene said. "I don't need you to defend me. I'm not going home. I'm going to school and raising the baby by myself."

The comment brought laughter from all the girls.

"You *are* kidding!"

"No, I'm not."

"They brought you to the wrong place! You belong down the street at the funny hospital!" Gloria said. "Really, I'm not trying to be mean, but you can't just strap a baby to your back and march off into the world!"

"But that's what I intend to do!" Jolene replied. She rung out the last cloth and bracing herself, she stood up.

Patricia came to the door. "Jolene."

The girl turned, wiping her wrinkled hands on her already wet dress.

"There's someone upstairs to see you."

Jolene froze. They'd found her.

"Who? My mother? Who?"

Patricia led her into the hall by the elbow. "It's him," she whispered. "*Him.*"

"Russell?"

"Yes."

"Why?"

"I don't know, but Jolene, listen to me carefully. Don't go up there crying, or with your hopes up. Go to your room, change your clothes and take a deep breath. Then go see him."

"Better he see me as I am. You know, how things really are," she said.

Jolene labored up the stairs to the front lobby in her wet work dress and unkempt hair.

How unprepared to see him she was! She almost burst into tears and ran into his arms, but she didn't.

He stood there, in the middle of the visiting room. After a quick glance at her swollen belly, he lowered his eyes and sat down. She sat across from him at arms length, looking him over, feeling a lump forming in her throat.

He looked much the same; same clothes she remembered, his hair the same, but he had grown a beard and mustache, making him appear older.

Without looking up, he handed her a small package. It was wrapped in paper her mother often used and it smelled like home.

"It's from my mother?"

He nodded.

"You saw her?"

"No. She gave it to me when I took you away. I forgot to give it to the nuns. It's been haunting me all this time."

"So, that's why you came."

She opened it and began to cry. At first softly, with just tears rolling down her face, but then as she turned it around in her hands and brought it to her nose, smelling the familiar odor of home, she sobbed.

Patricia, who'd been standing at the doorway, came to her. "What is it?"

"It's my book, Tess. She had it hidden all this time. You see, she knew I didn't belong there. My mother knew, and that's why she saved this, and that's why she let you take me away, Russell. Russell, aren't you ever going to look at me?"

He lifted his head.

"Don't you understand this? My ma knew she couldn't burn this book. It was too much a part of *me*."

Russell didn't answer. Again, he lowered his eyes.

"You really don't understand," Jolene said softly and sadly.

After many painfully quiet moments, he spoke. "I got a job in a town south of Knoxville. Rented me a house. You'd like it, Jolene, a whole lot."

He looked up to find her watching him, a little bewildered.

"There's a screened-in porch in the back where you can watch the sun come up. A milk truck comes by twice a week. Milk for our baby."

Then she smiled, a little.

"I built a chicken coop so we can have eggs every day."

He went to her, burying his head against her breast.

"How could you have left me like this?" she cried.

"Forgive me," he said.

"I love you."

"I love you."

"Why did you leave me?" she whispered.

"Please, don't ask me that."

"I need to."

"I was...afraid, really for the first time in my life, I was afraid."

"And now?"

"I can't live without you. You gave me something I never had. Hope. You were so strong, living there with those crazy people. It didn't change you. You knew who you were."

"I was confused, a lot. I'm still not sure about so many things. But I know I love you. That I know."

He took her face in his hands. "Jolene, you got more spunk than anyone I've ever met in my damn miserable life. Woman, you can have all the books I can afford to buy you!"

26

Bonnie was supposed to be preparing potato pancakes for the social. Instead, she wandered stoic through the autumn woods, missing her daughter.

It'd been a year. There was never peace for her, not knowing if Jolene had pulled through. The girl was never searched for or mourned over. As everyone could plainly see, she'd run off with Russell Nash. It must have been all planned out how they would steal the car and cross the county line. No one asked the unanswerable question: Why did she handle the snakes?

Arliss was the only one who had any idea what went on, but he said nothing about it. He was married off to Penny. She was happy to be a wife, wanting children, cooking, sewing and doing all the things a Godly wife at The True Believers was destined to do. He was chosen to be her mate, without question. A cross for her to bear with sobriety and prayer.

As for Jolene, she was never mentioned again at The True Believers. It was forbidden. She never existed, the prophecy never existed. Like Walter Blair and the others, Jolene Mosley was a testament to failure, thrown into the rogue's gallery forever.

Bonnie wandered past the keeper's shed, not used since Russell occupied it. She went inside, remembering that he'd had no time to take his few possessions with him when he fled.

As she creaked the door open, she noticed something just under the edge of the bed.

She picked up an unfinished carving in a dark hickory. A wild mare with nostrils flared.

Bonnie remembered that Russell had told her, "Because I love her!"

The woman turned the horse over in her hands, feeling the chiseled grooves. There was great care taken with every detail.

She knew the carving was meant for Jolene, and she knew her daughter was alive.

Like she'd done with her daughter's precious book *Tess of the d'Urbervilles* years before, she went home, hid the half-finished mare away, where no one would discover it, then she went to the kitchen to make potato pancakes.

Mustn't be late for the social.

Printed in the United States
1284600001BA/55-102

9 781592 869626